"T" is for Antonia

Other books in the
Secret Keeper Girl Series

"T" is for Antonia

Dannah Gresh
author of Secret Keeper Girl

and Suzy Weibel

Moody Publishers

CHICAGO

All Scripture quotations, unless otherwise indicated, are taken from the *Holy Bible, New International Version*®. NIV®. Copyright © 1973, 1978, 1984 by International Bible Society. Used by permission of Zondervan. All rights reserved.

Interior design: JuliaRyan | www.DesignByJulia.com
Cover and illustrations: Andy Mylin
Some images: © 2008 JupiterImages Corporation

Library of Congress Cataloging-in-Publication Data

Gresh, Dannah.
  T is for AnTONia / Dannah Gresh and Suzy Weibel ; [illustrations, Andy Mylin].
    p. cm. -- (Secret Keeper Girl series)
  Summary: When sixth-grader Toni tries out for the boy's football league against her father's wishes and school rules, she finds herself in after-school detention, where she meets three other girls who join her in forming the "Secret Keeper Girl Club." Includes a mother/daughter Girl Gab assignment.
  ISBN 978-0-8024-8705-6
[1. Clubs--Fiction. 2. Middle schools--Fiction. 3. Schools--Fiction. 4. Football--Fiction. 5. Sex role--Fiction. 6. Christian life--Fiction. 7. Friendship--Fiction.] I. Weibel, Suzy. II. Mylin, Andy, ill. III. Title.
  PZ7.G8633Taai 2008
  [Fic]--dc22

                          2008026485

We hope you like this book from Moody Publishers. We want to give you books that help you think and figure out what truth really looks like. If you liked this and want more information, you and/or your mom can go to www.moodypublishers.com or write to . . .

Moody Publishers
820 N. LaSalle Boulevard
Chicago, IL 60610

1 3 5 7 9 10 8 6 4 2

Printed in the United States of America

To my mom, Sharon Dunton.
Sorry I didn't stay in the patent leather and lace for long.
But what an amazing and safe atmosphere of love
you raised me in. I love you!

S.W.

"T" is for Antonia

CHAPTER 1

They Can't Stop Me

I'm sorry, but there is **no way** they can stop me from doing this.

They can pour chocolate syrup into my ears while I sleep and then stick me in a freezer so the chocolate turns into Tootsie Rolls. I'm still going to do it.

I am trying out for the Rutherford B. Hayes Middle School football team.

Why wouldn't I play football? I have been in this amazing throwing and kicking contest for the past three years. Kids from all over the country compete. When I was nine years old, and last year when I was eleven, they even chose me to go to a real pro football game and compete at halftime. I could beat most of the boys in my age group, even though they always make me play in the girls' division.

I come from a family that eats, sleeps, and breathes football. My dad played for the Philadelphia Eagles.

But now he's the problem. All of a sudden he doesn't think that football is "appropriate for girls," to use his words.

"I think we'll have you take a break from *Kick and Throw, Junior Pro* this year," he said.

"What?" I just about dropped my cream soda on our new kitchen tile. Talk about getting hit by a train that you never saw coming!

"I was thinking that maybe we should give some of the other kids a chance to win." He winked at me.

"You're serious?" I was waiting for a laugh to follow, but it never did.

"Your mom and I have been talking and, well . . . it's just that you're not a little girl anymore."

"That's kind of the whole point, Dad. I'm in sixth grade. I can play middle school football this year." I had been waiting *forever* to be old enough to play football for my school—just like my brothers.

"What are you two talking about?" My mom was passing through the kitchen carrying a basket of laundry the size of Mount Rushmore. Poor Mom—she constantly has a mountain of dirty clothes attached to one hip or the other. Three kids playing sports year round will do that to a woman, I guess.

"We're discussing football," Dad said. I decided to try a quick exit. Something about the way Mom and Dad looked at each other was making me feel nervous about my future in football.

"Can I go ride my bike?" I asked. Anything to get out of wherever this conversation was going. I would have gladly hopped into the dentist's chair at that moment if the sound of a drill on my teeth could drown out Dad's next sentence.

"Just a minute, Toni." Dad sighed. He threw one last pleading glance at Mom, but she just nodded. "Your mom and I have given this a lot of thought, and . . ."

I know my dad finished his sentence like two seconds later, but it felt like he paused for hours. Long enough for me to see all my dreams die right before my eyes. My whole life I've wanted to play football for my school. I can just see it: I'm the only Shark (that's our mascot) standing between the guy with the football and a touch-down. If I don't tackle him, we lose. He thinks he's going to run right past me—after all, I'm just a girl, and a kicker at that. But he needs to think again, because before he can take even one more step I hit him hard and he goes down. The crowd explodes . . .

" . . . we think it might be best if you stick to soccer this fall," my dad finished.

"That's not fair!" I know it's such a little kid thing to do, but I stomped my foot.

"Temper tantrums won't get you anywhere, Big Foot." Somehow my brother Marcos, who is seventeen years old and on the high school football team, had managed to sneak into the kitchen without anyone seeing him. I could tell by the wicked grin on his face that he was enjoying this. He grabbed a can of pop out of the fridge and jumped up on our new granite countertop.

"Down" was all Mom said. Marcos obeyed her like a whipped little puppy, but that crooked smile was still plastered to his face. **Ooh**, that smile always makes me so mad that I can't think straight. But then Marcos took me completely by surprise.

"I think you guys should let her play," Marcos said. He emptied the can in one huge gulp and crushed it flat with one hand. I have to admit, Marcos's muscles are pretty impressive. I can barely fit two hands around his upper arm, and I have pretty big hands. I *can't* fit both hands around his neck. I should know. I have tried plenty of times.

"I mean, I'm one of the captains of the high school team, and Big Foot here's the future of Marion football." He hopped up on the counter again, but no one seemed to notice.

"Marcos, please don't call your sister Big Foot," my mom sighed.

I have always been way off the growth charts. Now, in sixth grade, I am already 5'9". One time the ladies' basketball coach from Ohio State saw my mom buying me shoes at the mall. She came all the way across the shoe store, gave my mom her business card, and told her to keep in touch. I was *four* years old. Marcos was tagging along that day, and I've been Big Foot ever since.

"Marcos, thank you for your input, but you are excused to go upstairs." Dad was looking at Marcos in that way that says he really means business.

"Sorry, Squirt." Marcos crossed his eyes at me as he passed. Then he leaned in close. "I really meant what I said," he whispered.

"Antonia, honey, come sit down." Mom had abandoned her laundry chores for the moment and was patting the yellow-and-green cushion on a dining room chair.

GO TO secretkeepergirl.com and type in the secret word "football" to see the real-life history of girls playing football!

11

"If it's okay with you, I think I'll stand," I said.

"Toni," my dad started again, "no one would ever argue your athletic ability. We have expected for a long time that you will play sports in college just like your brothers."

Marcos is not my only amazing athlete-brother. My oldest brother, Milo, plays college basketball. I was so wishing he was here to defend me.

"We know you are only twelve, Toni," Mom said, "but it's right around your age that things start changing for boys and girls."

"Like what?" I mumbled.

"Well, like boys and girls might begin to think of each other as more than just teammates." Mom looked to Dad for some help.

He cleared his throat. "There are physical changes that start to happen around your age," he said.

"Ew, Dad! That's **gross**!" There was no way my dad just said that out loud.

"Here's the thing, Toni," Dad continued. "We have made up our minds. You will not be playing football. It's just not appropriate anymore. After a good play—on the sidelines—we can't have your teammates giving you, um . . . the universal football sign for 'Good Job.'"

I threw up my hands and turned to my mom. "Can you please tell me what Dad just said? In English?"

My mom rarely blushes, but she suddenly turned as red as a beet. "They might pat you on the butt," she said.

Could my parents possibly scar me any more in one short afternoon? As soon as I could I escaped to the freedom of my bike, but no matter how fast I pedaled I couldn't escape the sound of my parents saying to me the most horrible word in the English language: *no*.

Then it occurred to me. No problema! I knew how to turn that "no" into a "yes" tomorrow. . . .

"T" is for Antonia

CHAPTER 2

Girls Can't Play

nem·e·sis [nem-uh-sis] an opponent or a rival whom a person cannot overcome

That's a new word we learned in school today, and I have decided that Trevor Kenworth is my nemesis. I *have* beaten him in every sporting event you can think of ever since kindergarten, but that never seems to sink in with him. He challenges me to races and games of HORSE on the basketball court, and one time he even challenged me to a fight! That one I said no to, but in everything else he ends up losing. I guess that's why he keeps trying.

Today when I arrived at school Trevor was the first person I saw. That is always a bad sign.

"So Diaz, you trying out for the football team?" He sneered.

"None of your business." I was trying to look cool as I stashed my books in my locker. Why was this leech hanging around anyhow?

"You know, my parents and I checked the rule book and it says it's illegal for a girl to play for the school." Trevor studied his fingernails casually, like he was just talking about the **weather** or something. I kind of wanted to peek at his fingernails to see if they were sharp and pointed and had slime oozing out of them.

"It's not *illegal*," I said. "You can go to jail for things that are illegal."

"I asked Coach Klutz, and he said girls can't play."

"That's an old rule, Trevor," I said. "Haven't you ever heard of Title Nine? Even Coach Klutz can't make rules that keep girls off of boys' teams."

Trevor shrugged. "Whatever," he said. And then he just walked off.

Fortunately, my first-period class is a study hall, and by the end of the hour I had developed a plan that would at least get me through tryouts . . . as a boy, if that's the way it had to be. I figured I could talk Coach Klutz out of his old-fashioned "no girls" rule *after* I made the team.

Coach has lunch duty on Fridays, so I was pretty sure his office would be empty. What I really needed to know was if the boys' locker room would be clear.

There's only one place to go when you need to know the boys' gym class schedule, and that's to Kate Harding. Her brother Pete and Marcos have always been on the same football team. We're not best friends or anything, but we talk. And I've found that if you need information on a boy, Kate is a good place to start.

"How could they have gym during lunch?" Kate asked me, twirling her hair around her finger. "Coach has lunch duty."

"So I can just go in and get what I need?" I asked.

"Yeah, I think so. But watch out for Miss Gilbert," she said.

I got chills thinking about Miss Gilbert, the girls' gym teacher, but I still pulled off Operation Football Equipment without a hitch. All of the equipment was laid out in neat piles for tryouts, and arranged by size. I grabbed a helmet, shoulder pads, a practice jersey, and some padded pants and was out of there in less than one minute.

I slid into the girls' locker room and stuffed everything into my locker. I was back in the lunchroom before anyone even noticed I had been gone. Kate gave me a double thumbs-up from across the room and I smiled.

During sixth period I pulled off the final part of my plan.

I waited until there were only ten minutes of math class left before the final bell rang, and then I raised my hand and tried to look desperate.

"Mr. Gulley, can I please use the bathroom?" I bounced a couple of times for added effect, hoping I wasn't over-doing it.

"Class will be over soon." Mr. Gulley looked at the clock. "Can't it wait?"

"No, sir, it really can't." Now I winced and turned up the acting heat.

"Do you have all of your assignments written down?" he asked.

"Yes, sir!" I grabbed my books and made a big deal of hurrying clumsily from the room. I think I should win an Oscar for my performance.

Ten minutes is not much time to put on a full foot-ball uniform. I fell down three times trying to pull up my stupid football pants. Suddenly I heard footsteps and voices and the truth hit me like a punch in the gut. The eighth grade girls' gym class was back, and there was no way I was getting out of there without being seen.

With no time to think, I threw on my helmet and began yelling and grunting like a guy, punching lockers,

and jumping on and off the locker room benches. I hoped the girls would think I was just some crazy football guy who was pumped up about the season and running through the girls' locker room on a dare. It worked.

The girls must have really thought I was out of my mind, because they totally jumped out of the way as I ran past them. Not only could I hear them laughing, but I could also hear Miss Gilbert's angry voice saying, "Young man, you come back here at once! Young man!"

I hid behind a huge trash bin for ten minutes, then managed to slip in quietly with a large group of excited football players headed for the field. For the second time today I felt really bad about what I had done. I never get in trouble.

After I make the team it will all be worth it, I told myself.

We reached the field and we each got down on one knee in front of Coach Klutz. I glanced at Trevor. He wasn't even paying attention to the coach. I set two goals for these tryouts. The first was to make the team. The second was to beat Trevor Kenworth in everything that we did on the field.

We ran forty-meter dashes. I beat Trevor.

We did a drill to work on moving our feet really fast.

Trevor fell down three times!

We hit the coaches like we were blocking. I could move them backward, but Trevor couldn't.

By the end of tryouts, I figured out that I am not the biggest, strongest, or best player around. But I'm not the weakest or worst either. And I know I am the best kicker. Coach began to divide us into two groups, and I could see right away that I was in the "good" group. I was going to make the team!

When I glanced at Trevor, who was in the other group, I couldn't believe what I saw. He had tears running down his cheeks. He was trying to slip his hand under his facemask and wipe them off so no one would notice. For a second, I actually felt bad for him.

Coach's voice brought me back to attention. "Boys, take a knee again. Good job. Good job. Go ahead and take those helmets off."

All around me the guys were taking off their helmets. Everyone's hair was wet and matted down. I could smell the combination of grass and sweat that I've come to know so well. It's not a bad smell. Turning my eyes back to the coach, I saw he was looking right at me.

"Take that helmet off, Son," Coach Klutz said.

"I'm fine, Coach." I tried to make my voice sound deep and confident.

"Son, I didn't ask how you were. I gave you instructions. Take your helmet off now."

I was aware that everyone was looking at me, and I was aware that it was dead silent on the field. I kept my helmet on.

"What's your name?" Coach was approaching me now.

"Toni, sir." I was really glad at this moment that my name is not something like Sissy, because my brain was mushy oatmeal.

"Tony, you did a nice job today, but that doesn't mean my rules don't apply to you. What grade are you in?" Coach was right in front of me now.

"Sixth, Coach," I answered.

"Sixth grade, hmm?" He stood above me flipping through the pages on his clipboard. "I don't see you on my list here, Tony. We must have missed you." He had his pen out. "What's your last name?"

I'm sorry I ever felt bad for Trevor Kenworth, because at that moment the little rat rose to his feet and aimed his skinny, pointed, slimy monster finger right at my face.

He spread his feet wide and tilted back his sweaty little head and announced to the whole team . . .

"That's Antonia Diaz, Coach!" Then he got so close to my face that I could smell the sloppy joes from lunch on his breath. "I was wondering why you wouldn't take off your helmet. I already told you this morning. *Girls* aren't allowed to play!"

I could tell by looking at Coach that I was in more trouble than any other student at Rutherford B. Hayes Middle School ever had been. I wondered what they'd do to me for punishment. Still, seeing as Coach's face had the look of a mad grizzly bear, I knew I wasn't going to have to wait to find out.

"T" is for Antonia

CHAPTER 3

Marcos Saves the Day

"Antonia, I'd like to see you in my office, please." I found Miss Gilbert waiting for me when I returned to the locker room. I shuffled in behind her like a puppy with its tail between the legs.

"Have a seat, Antonia." For a while we just looked at each other, but finally a smile cracked on her face. "Do you want to tell me what this is all about?" she asked, waving her hand toward the football uniform that I still wore. I figured Miss Gilbert was the last friendly face I was likely to see for a while, so I just let the whole story rip. I told her everything, even about Kate helping me get into the locker room during lunch (but I didn't mention Kate by name). Then I told her about all that had happened on the field, right down to Trevor Kenworth ratting me out to Coach Klutz. I *did* mention Trevor by name. He deserves it.

For a few seconds Miss Gilbert just kept on smiling and shaking her head. "Wow," she said. "Antonia, you have got some guts." Teachers are so weird sometimes.

"Am I in trouble?" I asked.

Miss Gilbert laughed. "Oh, I'm willing to bet the answer to that is going to be yes. Let's see, we've got you today on charges of breaking and entering, trespassing, theft, skipping class, and impersonating a male student."

I was frozen to my seat—stuck like a piece of chewing gum to the bottom of some kid's shoe. Miss Gilbert laughed again as she knelt down in front of me. She cupped my dirt-stained face in her hands and then ruffled my knotted, sweaty hair. Two hours in a football helmet does not produce a soft, manageable mane. "I think we can get you off easy since these were crimes of passion," she said, standing up again.

"What's a 'crime of passion'?" I asked.

She handed me a Kleenex. "A crime of passion is when you do something wrong, but it has been caused by strong emotions rather than a desire to be rebellious. You are guilty, yes, but I think we can find some mercy for you in this case."

I looked up to see Coach Klutz wander in. He leaned against the door and stood there looking at me.

"Do I have to tell my parents?" I asked Miss Gilbert, trying not to look in Coach's direction.

"Let me ask you this," she said. "How do you think it will go for you if they find out Monday morning through a phone call from Principal Butter?"

I groaned. "The dog will get my bed and I'll be sleeping on his little fleece thingy," I answered, ". . . in his doghouse."

As I headed out the door I gave Miss Gilbert a silent nod. She was pretty cool, I guess. Coach Klutz was leaning against the door frame. He moved to let me through. "Sorry, Coach," I said as I passed by him.

Just when I got to my locker I heard the coach's voice. "Hey, Diaz," he said, and I turned to face him. "I'd like to find a way to fix this. I'm not sure I want to lose a player like you."

For just one second, everything was right with my world again. Maybe he would go to the school board for me—it would be a meeting of huge importance. I could see all of my classmates marching outside the boardroom with their picket signs.

"Give Toni the boot! Let her kick for Rutherford B. Hayes!"
"We want Toni and that's no baloney!"

But I saw one other picture in my fantasy that brought me crashing back to reality even faster than I ran my sprints today—I saw Mom and Dad sitting in the back of that same board meeting, frowns painted on their unhappy faces. They had a sign too: *"They'll pat you on the butt."*

"Sorry, Coach." I sighed. "I'm pretty sure I've blown any chance I had of playing football for you . . . at least with my mom and dad."

I started the longer-than-ever walk out to the curb where my mom always picks me up after school. My shoes felt like they were made of cement. This trip to the car was probably the last walk I would take as a free woman for a very long time. In fact, I am probably still going to be grounded on my fortieth birthday.

My shadow disappeared from in front of me and I had to stop suddenly to keep from running into Trevor Kenworth and his greasy little sidekick, Bubba Bingam. It's hard to believe that those two puny weasels could actually block the whole sidewalk, but they did.

"Tough luck today, Diaz," Trevor said.

"Yeah, tough luck," Bubba echoed.

"You weren't even there, Bubba," I said. Bubba was about a fourth-string player on the school's huge soccer team. He never gets to play. "But, hey, I hear the soccer team is thinking of using you as a spare ball this year."

"He may sit on the bench," Trevor answered for Bubba, "but at least he's *on* the team. Oh, and I made the football team. Did you hear that?"

"*Que bueno*," I said, knowing he didn't understand Spanish. *Where is my mom?*

"How about you, Diaz? You playing any football this year?" He sneered.

Suddenly, before my very eyes, Trevor and Bubba were each lifted about one foot off the ground, their feet kicking slightly as they dangled helplessly in the hungry grip of the unseen monster behind them.

"*Hola*, boys," came the deep voice of Marcos. The terrified boys tried to turn their heads to see who it was that held them by the collar of their shirts, but Marcos was too strong.

"They bugging you, Squirt?" Marcos asked me.

"Nah, I can take care of them just fine," I said, and Marcos winked at me.

"Well, we need to get going. Say, where do you suppose we should dump these two punks?" Marcos said.

I just smiled and shrugged. I had never seen Marcos like this before—usually I was the one dangling two feet off the ground.

"Tell you what," Marcos suggested. "I think we need to put them over here where they will be safe from harm." Marcos moved toward some enormous bushes that tower like big ocean waves over a statue of our school mascot a few steps away from where we stood. He plopped one boy into each bush and then dusted off his hands.

"I'm starved, Squirt, what do you say?" And then Marcos offered me his arm like we were headed off to prom together. I hooked my arm inside of his and we laughed all the way to his car.

We laughed even harder as we pulled out of the school's circle drive, watching Bubba, who managed to escape first, trying to pull Trevor out of the second bush. We couldn't see Trevor's head at all, only two legs sticking out at weird angles.

Maybe this *was* going to be my last day of freedom. But Marcos made all of it bearable for me. Even if only for a day, Marcos stood up for me instead of rising up against me.

Maybe if Marcos came to school with me Monday as my bodyguard, I wouldn't be so afraid to face Principal Butter. I wasn't looking forward to that *at all*.

"T" is for Antonia

CHAPTER 4

Detention Blues . . . or Pinks

It doesn't surprise me that Miss Gilbert gave me a pink slip for three days of detention beginning this Wednesday. And it definitely doesn't surprise me that my parents grounded me for like a gazillion years. What *does* surprise me is that somehow the story of my tryout and Trevor's tattletale adventure has made it all around the school . . . and I am the hero! There are two petitions going around that have "Let Toni be a Shark!" printed across the top. I have never heard of most of the kids who have signed them. Both petitions insist that Trevor be removed from the team to make room for me.

"So what's the big idea, Diaz?" Trevor asked. He cornered me by the drinking fountain just before lunch.

"What do you mean?" I have never noticed before that Trevor's left eye twitches. It pulls his lip up into a weird crooked line.

"Don't play dumb," Trevor said. "You've seen the petitions."

"Yeah, but that's all," I said. "I didn't start them. And I didn't sign them, either."

"You need to stop them." Trevor licked his lips and looked around nervously.

"Trevor, I can't stop what I didn't start. And it doesn't even matter, okay? My parents won't let me play. You win." I held up my pink slip for extra proof that this argument was pointless.

"Hey, Toni—everything okay over here?" Smitty and Beast, two of the biggest eighth graders on the football team, walked over to where we stood.

"Yeah, it's fine, guys. We're good." I can't believe Smitty and Beast even know my name. These guys are middle school football legends.

"Get lost, weasel," Beast said, towering over Trevor.

"What are you going to do about it?" Trevor said.

"Are you serious? Beast, did he just threaten you?" Smitty asked.

Trevor didn't hesitate. "I want the petitions gone."

"What petitions?" Beast asked, as if he didn't know about them.

"I made the team fair and square," Trevor said.

"You made the team because you ratted on Toni,"

Smitty said. "She outplayed you and you were about to be cut. Is that fair and square?"

"She can't play!" Trevor was crying a little, and he raised his voice. A bunch of kids began to gather around, which was making me feel nervous. Trevor snatched the pink slip out of my hand and shoved it into Smitty's face. "Look! *I* made the team! *She* got detention!"

Beast snatched the slip from Trevor, flattening it back out against the leg of his jeans. He handed it to me without even looking at me.

"Okay, Kenworth, how about we make a deal. We'll get rid of the petitions and you can stay on the team—*if* you can prove you're a man," Beast said.

"He's twelve," I muttered under my breath.

"Meet us after lunch in the gym," Beast said. "Hope those skinny little arms can do some pushups, Kenworth."

He nodded at me and, just like that, our little meeting ended. Most of the crowd followed Smitty and Beast like love-struck little girls. Trevor and I walked off in different directions.

On my way to detention I watched the football team trudge out to the practice field in the rain. *At least I'm not the only one who is having the worst week ever*, I thought. Danika McAllister, one of the most popular girls in school, got detention for hitting Mrs. Hefty in the head with Purple Flurp, whatever that is. With a sigh, I entered day one of my detention assignment.

Detention this week is in Mrs. V's class. Mrs. Velasquez is probably the nicest teacher in the whole school. She doesn't talk down to us like we are little kids. She makes us feel respected, like we have something important to say.

"Hello, Toni," she greeted me as I walked in the room. I smiled. "Your name came up at the teachers' lunch table today."

No kid wants their name to come up at the teachers' lunch table.

"Someone presented us with a petition and asked if we would like to sign it," she said.

"Mrs. V, I'm sorry," I offered.

"Don't be." She winked at me. "I signed it. Oh, but I did add a note that Trevor has to be allowed to play as well."

It wasn't until this moment that I realized Kate Harding was in the room with me. Danika was there, too, I guess for the Flurp thing. She should try out for softball this spring. It was a good throw, even though she says she didn't mean to do it.

Mrs. V signed my pink slip and told me I could sit any-where in the room. "Make yourself at home," she said, and smiled.

"May I use a computer?" I asked. She nodded, and I leaned down to Kate on my way to grab a laptop. "You in here because of me?"

"Nope. I did this all on my own," she said. Kate always makes me smile.

I logged on to my chat account and hoped as hard as I could that my big brother Milo was online. It's killing me that I haven't been able to talk to him about my foot-ball problems. Plus, I feel so bad about upsetting Mom and Dad. They almost cried while they were grounding me. I don't know. Sometimes I just need my Milo.

Seeing his chat icon pop up on the screen was even better than the fireworks at the Sky Pop fireworks show last Friday night. "**Yes!**" I said, a little louder than I wanted to, which made everyone in the room turn and look at me.

"Sorry," I said.

Another girl had come in—I hear she's from Africa

somewhere. All the kids say she's the one who pulled the fire alarm on Monday.

By the time I looked back down, Milo had already noticed I was online.

U Know Milo: *Hey Chica, que pasa?*

T for Antonia: *I'm in detention.*

U Know Milo: *Mom and Dad told me. lol*

T for Antonia: *Yeah, not funny. Can you believe how lame my life is?*

U Know Milo: *Bad week. But hey, ur a soccer guru! Play on!*

T for Antonia: *I don't want to play sccr if I can't play ftball.*

U Know Milo: *Why not play a sport u can play your whole life?*

T for Antonia: *???*

U Know Milo: *Even if u play in H.S. u won't play college ftball.*

T for Antonia: *U siding w them?*

U Know Milo: *Just looking out for my lil sis.*

T for Antonia: *Way 2 b there 4 me.*

U Know Milo: *I'm the pres of your fan club, right?*

Milo's right. He has always been my number one fan. He talked Mom out of making me enter the Miss Teeny Pop contest when I was five. He wears number 51 on his college basketball team because it's *my* number. That's why what I did next will probably haunt me for a long time.

T for Antonia: *Not anymore. U R FIRED!*

And I signed off.

While I was staring at the screen in front of me, Kate and Danika walked over to Yuzi and me. Kate was really excited. "Toni! Yuzi! Do you want to be in a girls-only club with me and Danika?" That's when I realized that "Yuzi" is the African girl's name.

"It's gonna be totally cool. Right, Danika?" she said.

"Totally!" Danika was excited, too. "We're going to call it the *Secret Keeper Girl Club*! We'll all promise to be true friends who don't blab each other's secrets to anyone else. Mrs. V even said we can have club meetings here in her art room Wednesdays after school."

"Soooo . . . what do ya think?" Kate asked hopefully.

"Yeah, I'm in," I said. I tried to smile, but I didn't feel like it just yet.

Milo ditched me, so here's hoping these new friends won't.

39

"I" is for Antonia

CHAPTER 5

I've Been Sharked

What sort of alien forces have taken over my life? Seriously—my dad, who has been my lifelong football coach, has decided he does not want me playing the sport. My brother Marcos, who has always been such a bully, is super-supportive. And my big brother Milo, who is supposed to be my number one fan, has totally stabbed me in the back. The way things are going right now, I would not be surprised if Mrs. V suddenly sprouted a tall black pointy cap, began to laugh wickedly, and tried to pedal away with my dog in her bike basket.

The best part of my week has been detention, since I got invited into the *Secret Keeper Girls Club*. I've never been in a girls' club before, but it looks like this is going to be pretty cool, even though we're all so . . . I don't know. Different. Dad and Mom even said that since the SKG Club meetings are gonna be advised by a teacher, they wouldn't be included in my grounding. Cool!

Today I was telling Mrs. V about my football woes when the other girls came bouncing into the room. Yuzi joined me at Mrs. V's desk. I found out she's not actually from Africa. She was born in the United States just like me. But her parents are Nigerian.

"May I sit with you?" she asked as she approached the desk. Yuzi says everything properly—the way teachers are always trying to get the rest of us to talk, only Yuzi does it naturally. Mrs. V smiled and I patted a space on the countertop next to me. Yuzi eagerly jumped up and sat with her legs crossed beside me.

"So, Toni, you were saying?" Mrs. V asked, turning back toward me. I saw Yuzi's eyebrows narrow like she was concentrating very hard on what I was going to say.

I picked up the paintbrush I had been playing with earlier, tickling myself under the chin as we talked. "So," I continued, "I have no idea what I am going to do until basketball season starts. I don't know if I'm good at anything besides sports." I looked up at the fluorescent lights and continued to run the paintbrush along the side of my neck. It sent shivers down my arms.

"I want to find out if there's anything else out there,"

I said, "but every time I think about it, I get stuck. I don't know where to start!"

Suddenly I saw Yuzi fold in two laughing, and her whole body rocked back and forth. Mrs. V covered her mouth with her hand, her eyes big and round. "Wow, Toni!" was all I heard from Kate in the back of the room, and Danika stared at me with her mouth open wide enough for a truck to drive through.

At that very moment I realized there was a sensation of cold and wet upon my neck. "Um, I just painted myself, didn't I?" I looked down to see the clean paintbrush I was holding earlier sticking out from underneath Yuzi's leg, while in my hand I held a large brush covered with bright orange paint.

"Yessss!" Yuzi squealed loudly, while the rest of the room erupted in laughter. I jumped off the counter and began to chase Kate and Danika with the orange paintbrush, while Yuzi and Mrs. V pretended to hide behind the desk for protection.

Mrs. V sent me to the girls' bathroom to get myself cleaned up. As I passed by the main offices, Principal Butter burst through the glass doors and stopped directly in front of me. "Miss Diaz, aren't you serving your second day of detention this afternoon?"

"Yes, sir," I answered. I had a difficult time stopping the giggles that were bubbling up inside of me. I imagined painting something on the perfect canvas of Principal Butter's shiny bald head. Maybe our school mascot, Sharkey.

"Do you find detention amusing, Miss Diaz?" Principal Butter frowned.

"No, sir." I still fought the giggles. "I just really need to get this paint washed off before it dries."

I pictured a fat, drooling Saint Bernard painted on the top of his head.

"It tickles, sir," I blurted in a fit of giggles. "Please, may I go?"

Principal Butter stepped to the side to let me go, and I could hear him calling after me as I entered the bathroom. By this time I was roaring at the thought of a big, blue M&M guy right on the top of Principal Butter's head. "No more painting in detention, Miss Diaz! This is not meant to be a holiday for you!"

I returned to the art room to find that my new best buds and Mrs. V had a surprise for me. "Look!" Kate said as I joined them. "We've been thinking about some other things you can try out for this fall besides sports." She handed me a slip of paper. It was filled with words written in marker. Each word was in a different color, and a lot of them had cute little drawings, too.

I gratefully took the list from Kate and began to read it aloud.

FALL MUSICAL

"I just don't know if I can get up and sing in front of a bunch of people," I said.

"You can be in the chorus," Danika offered.

"Yeah, but you still have to sing a solo to try out," I said. "And you have to dance. I look like a chicken when I dance."

"You could always audition doing the Chicken Dance!" Mrs. V said. We booed and hissed Mrs. V's bad joke, but we were laughing all the same.

FLAG SQUAD

"Okay, who put this one on the list?" Everyone was chuckling, trying to hide their glee at this obviously mismatched suggestion. "Can you honestly see me in one of those glittery tank tops spinning a flag?"

"Sometimes they twirl rifles," Kate said, and she and Danika fell into fits of giggles.

SCHOOL MASCOT

"This one is my favorite for you, Toni," said Mrs. V. "I think a mascot needs to be very athletic. You would make a fearsome shark!"

"That's true," said Yuzi. "And a mascot needs to have a sense of humor, and maybe be a little mischievous."

"You'd be an awesome shark," Danika chimed in. Kate was nodding her head in agreement.

"Wow, I wouldn't have thought of trying out for mascot in a million years, but you're right. It's dance and theater and sports all rolled into one," I said.

"Let's find out when auditions are," said Kate. I'm learning that when Kate gets excited, sparks fly. She grabbed my arm and pulled me into the hallway. After checking that Principal Butter was nowhere in sight, she pulled me all the way over to the announcement board by the main offices. And there it was:

ATTENTION RBH STUDENTS: Auditions for the school mascot, Sharkey, will be this coming Monday after is for Antonia

school in the gymnasium. Be prepared to perform one skit and one dance in the Sharkey costume. And remember—all potential sharks must be able to complete at least 35 pushups! See you there!

I felt three hands on my shoulder as I turned to face my Secret Keeper Girl sisters. They were looking at me with wide eyes and even wider smiles.

"Good thing you don't have detention Monday," Yuzi said.

"T" is for Antonia

CHAPTER 6

Mascot Madness

This was without a doubt the dumbest idea I have ever had. Toni Diaz a mascot? Why would I think this had anything other than disaster written all over it?

Before I could make up a dance, I needed to choose my music. Yuzi came to my house to help, and after we watched a couple Saturday morning cartoons, we got right to work.

"What we need," Yuzi explained, "is something fun and spirited, but also a lot simpler than it sounds. No offense, but you are a rookie, right?"

"If rookie means hopeless, then yes," I said.

"Stop it!" Yuzi gave me a playful shove. "We can't have that attitude, young lady shark! I just meant you haven't danced before. Now, we want to pick music that stands out from what the others will use."

"Everyone else will use hip-hop," I said.

"Exactly! That's why I brought these." Yuzi reached into her bag and tossed about ten CDs on my bed.

"Wow, you actually use CDs? That's very old school of you," I teased.

"These, Toni, are my mom's Nigerian CDs," she said.

"You mean like tribal music?" I asked.

"No, it's kind of like reggae and pop. Here, listen." Yuzi grabbed my laptop and threw the CD in. I still thought it sounded like African tribal music, but it was pretty cool. It was definitely dance music.

GO TO secretkeepergirl.com and type in the secret word "Music" to hear the Nigerian music Toni and Yuzi picked!

By lunchtime Yuzi had taught me some easy moves, and we both agreed that Sharkey would look hilarious doing the dance. We could barely get through it without cracking up. Even my mom came in to see our masterpiece, and she left the room crying from laughing so hard. We had a hit on our hands.

After we ate the grilled cheese sandwiches and tomato soup that my mom made for us, we headed back upstairs to tackle the skit. During lunch we had decided to base the skit around our number one football rival, the Riverside Pirates.

"Okay," said Yuzi, "what are pirates known for?"

"You mean other than getting crushed by Shark football?" I asked.

Yuzi rolled her eyes. "You have to think like a mascot now," she said. "Mascots don't win or lose. They just entertain."

"I'd rather hit people than entertain them," I said. I saw Yuzi's horrified look. "I mean in *football!*"

"I can be the pirate for you," Yuzi offered. "I'll dress up in a pirate costume and you can make me walk the plank or something."

"Yuzi, that's perfect!" I squealed. "You can wear an eye patch and we'll put a fake bird on your shoulder."

"I'll have a coat hanger coming out of *me* sleeve like a hook!"

I laughed at Yuzi's pirate accent. "And I can be circling underneath the gangplank, just waiting for you to fall in!" I added.

"*Aaargh!*" Yuzi growled. "And I'll poke you with *me* hook!"

When my dad got home we convinced him to help out with the audition, too. His pickup truck would be the pirate ship, and he said he would make a "gangplank" that came off the tailgate.

Just before Yuzi's parents arrived to pick her up, we called Kate and Danika to tell them our plans. "Now *that* would be a great skit for the Miss Teeny Pop contest!" Danika said with awe in her voice. Both promised to come watch the auditions Monday afternoon. I fell into bed that night so satisfied with my new friends and the hope of becoming a *new* Toni Diaz—*Mascot Extraordinaire!*

It was impossible to focus during any of my classes. I was so nervous that I couldn't even eat lunch, and I don't mind admitting that lunch is my all-time favorite school subject. After school I met Yuzi and my dad at the gate that leads to the track and football field. My dad is amazing. He spent all day painting his truck with washable paint. He made it look like an old wooden ship, and he even took a big Styrofoam ball, painted it black, cut it in half, and made it look like the "ship" had been hit by a couple of cannonballs.

"Daddy, thank you!" I threw my arms around my dad's massive neck. He picked me up and swung me through the air just like he's done ever since I was a little girl.

"Anything for my princess," he said. I rolled my eyes, but the truth is I love it when he calls me that.

The dance part of my audition went perfectly. I was insanely grateful for the big shark costume that hid my identity, since the guys were practicing football just fifty yards away. As I finished the last part of the routine, I looked up into the stands. Through the tiny slits that make up Sharkey's eyes, I saw Kate and Danika whooping and jumping up and down.

Right on cue my dad drove his pickup onto the track behind me, and Yuzi, in full costume and totally acting the part of a pirate, hopped out. The small audience in the stands roared for her.

Yuzi and I both jumped up on the back of the pickup truck. We had a short sword fight that ended with Yuzi losing her sword. Then I struck a very bossy pose and pointed at the gangplank. Yuzi looked scared and shook her head *no*.

I nodded my Sharkey head up and down. *Yes!*

Finally, I grabbed Yuzi and I pretended to force her onto the plank. She bit her nails in fear—the nails on her left hand, that is. Her right hand was a perfectly formed coat-hanger hook.

I jumped to the ground and began circling under the plank while the sound guy, also right on cue, began playing scary music from an old movie called *Jaws*. My mom helped me download the song. She told me it played every time the movie shark was about to chomp somebody's arm off. Yuzi paced back and forth; I could tell she loved doing this.

And that's when the sky fell. Or, that's when a football fell *from* the sky. I've always said Trevor can't kick a football to save his life. His sorry attempt at a field goal drilled poor Yuzi right in her little pirate head, and before she could regain her balance she fell on top of Sharkey, which happened to be *me*.

I keep playing the moment over and over again in my head. Me looking up to see Yuzi falling, Yuzi looking petrified, Yuzi putting out her hands to brace herself. And Yuzi's coat-hanger hook ripping through the clean gray fabric of Sharkey's custom-made, very expensive belly.

As I lay in the grass, Yuzi was squirming to get off of me and the crowd laughed uncontrollably. No one laughs at sharks. Maybe I'm more of a clown fish.

I'm never gonna hear the end of this! I thought.

"T" is for Antonia

CHAPTER 7

Chicana Power

If it was only Sharkey's costume that suffered from that fall, I think I would laugh, too. But it took a good three minutes to get me back on my feet because Yuzi's hook-hand was buried wrist-deep in the belly of my costume. This allowed enough time for the football team to rush to the fence in order to see what the commotion was all about.

As soon as I lifted the shark's toothy head off my shoulders, the entire team began to point and laugh. Trevor, whose terrible kick caused all of the excitement, led the way.

"Nice work, Diaz!" he hooted. "I had no idea you had so many talents."

Oh, how I wish the teeth in Sharkey's head were real.

"I was just wondering," he continued, "do you think you could throw me our football? It seems to have landed near your *ship*." A bunch of the guys laughed.

"That's because you can't kick," I growled in return. "You hit Yuzi in the head!"

"How do you know I wasn't *trying* to do that?" He smiled, but it was a mean smile. The kind you might expect to see on an alligator just before it rips into its prey.

"I've seen you kick, that's how," I said. "If you actually hit what you aimed at, then today is a first."

"All right you two, knock it off." Coach Klutz stepped between us on Trevor's side of the fence and smiled in my direction. "You still sitting this season out, Diaz?" he asked.

"Yes, sir." I looked down and kicked the gravel at my feet.

"That's too bad," Coach said. "We sure could use you." He glanced quickly at Trevor and then sent the football team back to their practice field. The truth is, Trevor's not actually a *horrible* kicker. It's just so hard to like the kid because he can't keep his mouth shut. Sure enough, after taking about ten steps back toward the field Trevor had to turn around again and have the last word.

"Diaz, we still need the ball," he said. "How about you just flip it to me with your little shark fins!"

I walked as slowly as I could to the football lying by my dad's truck. Yuzi went to pick it up, but I shook my head *no* and she understood. Still moving slowly, just to irritate Trevor, I slipped out of Sharkey's tattered costume and picked up the football. I made solid eye contact with Trevor, and then I booted that football in a straight, high spiral right into the middle of the practice field. From the sidelines where they were lined up for sprints, Smitty and Beast and a bunch of other guys threw their fists in the air and shouted, "Whooo!" Then they started chanting, "Toni! Toni! Toni!"

Trevor scowled at me, but at least for now he was done shooting off his mouth.

Dad laughed the whole way home.

We pulled into the driveway and my heart sank even further. There was Milo's little yellow pickup truck. I felt a wave of nausea thinking of the last words I had spoken to him: *You're fired.*

Dad was still lost in his joy over the events of the afternoon. "Oh man," he said with a huge smile as he exited the truck. "I think it's going to be a long time before I laugh this hard again. Please tell me someone caught that on camera."

I looked at him in horror. "If that gets out on video I'll **never** be able to show my face again!" I said.

"If what gets out on video?" Milo and Marcos emerged from the garage, sweaty from a game of basketball on the backyard court. Milo grabbed me and gave me a big squeeze, as if nothing had ever happened between us.

"Your sister made mascot history today," Dad said, and he proceeded to tell the entire humiliating story all over again as all three guys laughed and held their sides.

"Dude, I am so posting that video tonight," Marcos said. "Dustin's mom was in charge of that tryout, I think. I'm gonna go call him. Way to go, Big Foot!"

He acted like I had just won a state playoff game or something. But I hadn't. All I did was embarrass myself in front of the entire football team and all of the other mascot wannabes. Again I felt a wave of longing pass through me—*why can't I just kick for the football team?*

My dad followed Marcos into the house, leaving me alone with Milo. "You want to go play catch, Mija?" he asked.

"I guess." I shrugged. I followed him through the garage and into our fenced backyard. Philly and Eagle, our overly hyper Dalmatians, jumped against me with delight as I emerged from the garage carrying a football.

I threw a couple of old tennis balls to the far corner of the yard and watched as the dogs sailed gracefully over the grass.

"So why did you come home?" I asked.

"I thought I'd hang out with you a little bit," he said.

"It's the middle of the week," I said. "Don't you have classes?"

"You want to know a secret about college?" he asked.

"What?"

"Well, first of all, all of my classes have like three hundred people in them," he said.

I could feel my eyes getting big. "Whoa," I said. "That's like a whole school almost."

"Yeah," he said. "No one really notices when you're gone."

"I'll bet you skip a lot of classes then," I said. I threw the tennis balls for Eagle and Philly again, this time into the swimming pool. The dogs splashed headfirst into the cold water.

"No skipping," he said, and he motioned for me to back up a little so we could throw the football. "If you miss a lot of classes in college you won't pass. That's like an unwritten rule."

"So you put your college career in jeopardy to come see me," I teased him.

Thwap. The tight spiral Milo threw hit me squarely in the hands.

"Pretty much." He grinned.

"Maybe I should give you back your job as fan club president then," I said, still feeling pretty bad about how I treated him my first day in detention.

"I humbly accept." Milo gave a low bow. "So . . . as president of your fan club I have to ask, what is your next move?"

I tossed the ball back to him. "Don't know," I said.

"Soccer?" he asked, and I noticed that his eyes looked hopeful.

"Nope." I shook my head defiantly.

"See, Toni, that's what I don't get," Milo said. "It's like you were created to be an athlete. Why are you running from it?"

"I'm not," I said. "I'm going to play basketball and softball. But there has to be more to me than sports."

"There's a *lot* more to you than sports," Milo said. "You're smart, you're funny. In fact . . ."

Milo's eyes got wide and he began bobbing his head up and down like he was about to bust a big dance move. I knew exactly what was coming. I struck a wide pose with my feet, put my hands on my knees, and moved my head the same way.

"What do I see?" Milo shouted.

"Hispanic panic!" I shouted back.

"What do I need?" Milo was even louder now.

"A Diaz, plee-az!" I matched him.

"And what do I know?" Milo roared.

"This chica can beat ya!"

"Hey—some people actually have homework to do!" Marcos stuck his head out of his second-story window, and he looked more than just a little irritated. But Milo and I were not to be quieted. Milo picked me up and ran, with me on his shoulders, to a spot directly underneath Marcos's window.

"Chicana power!!!"

Our voices lifted in unison, with fists raised high in the air, were met by the perfect aim of Marcos . . . and a full bucket of ice-cold water landing on our heads.

"T" is for Antonia

CHAPTER 8

Rubber Ducky

If someone had told me a month ago that Danika McAllister and I would be friends—that I would be calling her cell phone and actually talking to her—I would never have believed it. I mean, Kate's favorite rock star, Alayna Rayne, and I were more likely to become friends than Danika and me.

Still, here she was, picking up my call on its second ring.

"Hi, Toni!" Danika's been having a tough time lately. All of her old friends, the popular crowd, have pretty much disowned her. Those girls can make it really hard on you when they decide they don't like you.

"I'm hoping you can hook me up with a favor," I said.

"Sure!" she said. "So what's your favor?"

"Well, I've been looking at the list you made for me in detention last week . . ."

"Sweet!" Danika said. "You gonna try something else?"

"I think I want to try out for the school musical," I said, almost with a question in my voice.

"Toni, that's awesome!" Danika said. "Tell me that's the favor you want! I'll coach you to get ready."

"That's the favor," I said.

"This is so cool. Can you come over after school tomorrow?" she asked me.

"I think so," I said. "I'm still grounded, but since it's a school thing, I think my mom will want me to try out and everything. Tomorrow's the only day we have. Tryouts are Wednesday."

"But that's club day," Danika said.

"I know. It's just that this is something I have to do."

"All right," she said. "Let's do it."

I'm not as bad at singing as I thought I would be. At least that's what Danika said, and she should know because she's had singing lessons. She sings in front of people all the time.

"Are you sure about the song?" I asked.

"Positive. Look, it's *You're a Good Man, Charlie Brown*, right?" I nodded. I needed to hear this logic again.

"And all the characters in that play are kids, right?" she said.

"Well, Snoopy's technically a *dog*," I pointed out. I just felt like arguing. Maybe it would get me out of singing . . .

"*Rubber Ducky*'s the perfect song!" Danika threw her hands up in the air like she had just solved the world's hunger crisis.

"For a **Muppet**!" I whined.

"Toni, trust me on this." Danika put an encouraging hand on my shoulder. "You need to do something that will make you stand out. It's like my voice coach always says: You don't want to be forgettable."

Danika made me sing that stupid song about twenty times before I went home. I had to sing while jumping rope, sing to a stuffed animal, sing at the top of the huge balcony that looks down on the McAllisters' living room, and sing while playing some video guitar game down in the basement. "This way you'll never forget the words. Plus, it makes your movements look a lot more natural," she explained.

How can anyone look natural while singing, "You make bath time lots of fun" to a stuffed hippopotamus? But she's right. I'll *never* forget the words to *Rubber Ducky*.

I was hoping tryouts would be in the music room, but since some of the rented props for the musical have already arrived, they decided to have auditions onstage. I was relieved to see Mindi Stewart, a girl I've played club basketball with for about four years, looking over her sheet music on the stage near the piano.

"Hey, Mindi," I said, trying to be casual and cool about the whole thing.

"Toni Diaz, are you serious?" Mindi smiled that huge smile she is famous for. She smiles when she fouls, when she gets fouled, and last year when she dislocated her finger she even came off the floor smiling at the fact that her finger was pointing in entirely the wrong direction. I needed that smile today.

"I'm trying out." I shrugged my shoulders.

"Sa-weet! I didn't know you did theater."

"Neither did I." I laughed. "I just need to try something new."

"You're going to love it!" Mindi smiled.

"Yeah. I'm really nervous," I told her.

"Aw, I was, too, the first year. You want to know the secret?" she asked me.

I thought I knew this one. "Picture everyone in their underwear?"

"Ew, gross!" She giggled. "No, see, you don't want your first time onstage to be just you, singing all alone. What you should do is find a place up here where you can sit unnoticed and be really close to the action. It'll help a lot when it's your turn."

I looked around on the stage and noticed that Snoopy's doghouse had already arrived. It had a flat roof, was hollowed out inside, and had white picket fencing attached on both sides.

"How about behind the doghouse?" I asked Mindi.

"That's perfect!" Mindi said, and her smile lit the stage.

It was a great plan. The first four kids who tried out were okay, but three of them sang the same song. I was beginning to see the wisdom in Danika's advice to be unique.

The only problem with my location was that if I peeked over the top of the doghouse I could be seen, but from inside the doghouse I could only see shadows. Mindi was onstage next, and I really wanted to see everything that she did. I needed some ideas about how to move when it was my turn to sing.

I snuck out of the doghouse and crawled along behind the picket fence to a place that gave me a perfect view. About halfway through Mindi's song my right leg, which I had been squatting on, fell asleep. I shifted my weight over to the left leg. The movement somehow dislodged the rubber ducky that was in the front pocket of my hoodie, and I watched it clatter to a stop about three feet in front of the picket fence. If that wasn't bad enough, it's a motion sensitive toy, so it flashed and quacked every time Mindi moved toward it.

Reaching through the fence I found that my arms were *just* too short to reach the duck. I mean centimeters short. I thought if I could just get my shoulder through the gap in the fence it would give me the extra length I needed.

Quack. Quack. Blink. Flash.

I pushed extra hard. One more millimeter . . . and then it **happened**. Not only did my whole shoulder manage to get through the fence, but my head went through as well. And there I was. Center stage, head stuck in a white picket fence, my fingers wrapped around a blinking, quacking rubber ducky, laughter rippling throughout the entire auditorium.

And for the first time since I had met her, Mindi Stewart was not smiling.

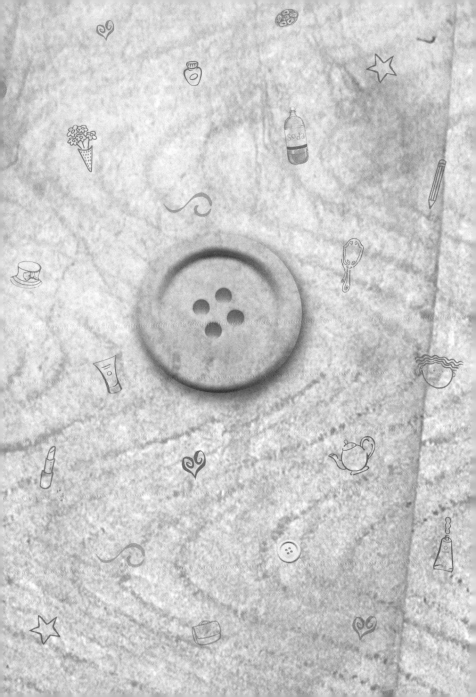

"T" is for Antonia

CHAPTER 9

Another Career

I burst into Mrs. V's classroom and slammed the door behind me. Leaning breathlessly against the wall, I tried to drown out the sound that was still ringing in my ears. Laughter—people laughing at me. I have been hearing that sound far too often this week. Hopefully, my Secret Keeper Girl sisters wouldn't laugh at me.

Suddenly it occurred to me . . . *where is everyone?* Danika did say that today was the first day of club, didn't she?

Then I saw them. Eight eyeballs peering at me from behind a long table in the back of the room. Or should I say four pairs of eyes? After all, they were attached to the faces of my new friends and Mrs. V. They seemed surprised to see me.

"How did your audition go?" Danika was the first to pop up. She had a look of high expectation on her face.

I felt my own face fall. "I didn't do it."

"What? Why not?" Danika looked shocked.

"Well, I was . . . hey, what are you guys doing back there?" I asked.

Approaching the table I found myself feeling a lot of regret that I hadn't just come here to begin with. It was awesome. Underneath the table was what I can only describe as paradise. The floor was laid with carpet pieces that were white, fluffy, and soft looking. Icicle lights, the kind people put on their roofs at Christmas, hung from the edges of two large square art tables that were pushed together. It looked like a gigantic girls-only fort! There were big, soft, comfy pillows all over the furry rugs, a couple of stuffed animals for emotional support, and a *ton* of yummy food to eat. Since I didn't eat lunch, I was starving.

"Wow," I whispered.

Without another word we all sank down onto the warm, white carpet. Mrs. V patted the spot next to herself, and as I crawled toward her I picked up a mushy, deep red pillow and two homemade chocolate chip cookies.

"So what happened, Toni?" Danika asked.

As I told the story, everyone munched on junk food and listened like I was reading their favorite bedtime story or something. There were a lot of reactions—like Yuzi choking on her Cheesy Chips when the ducky fell out of my pocket and rolled onstage, and Kate screaming, "Oh no you didn't!" when I talked about my head popping through the fence. Mrs. V comforted me with pats on the back when I talked about how the drama teacher had to use actual tools to remove one slat of the rented fence to set my head free, and Danika fumed over how some of the same girls who have been messing with her, especially Laney Douglas, stood pointing and laughing at me the whole time.

"Don't worry about them, Toni," she said. "They are so not worth it."

"I've never been this embarrassed in my life," I said miserably.

"Where is Sharkey's costume when you need it?" Yuzi said with a little grin on her face.

"I know, right?" I said.

Danika soon called our first official Secret Keeper Girl club to order. We started talking about the new club rules—which would include "No wearing of costumes!" Then, we ended up talking about other things, which made me happy. Enough of my try-out troubles—I'm done!

Kate and I walked out to the parking lot together after club. "So what's next, Toni?" she asked me.

"Well, I think I'm done with performing," I said, and we both laughed. "Thanks, by the way. I feel a ton better after club."

"I totally want to go after Laney and her little groupies," Kate said. "They are **so** stinking mean!"

"I don't care about them," I said.

"Are you serious?" Kate asked.

"I still have no idea what I'm good at. Or if I'm good at anything," I said.

"Oh please," Kate said, "you're like the best athlete in our class!"

I shook my head. "There has to be something more, Kate."

"Danika said you're a good singer," Kate offered. I shrugged.

We plopped on the curb to wait for our moms, which made my digital camera fall out of my backpack. Kate caught it just before it hit the pavement.

"Hey, Toni, these are really good!" Kate said. She was looking at the photos on my camera. "Where are these from?"

"Oh, Milo came home this week and we went hiking. I don't usually take my camera, but I got some good shots, huh?" I leaned in and looked over her shoulder.

"Toni, these are more than good," Kate said. "These are amazing. In fact . . ."

Suddenly Kate sprang to her feet and grabbed the shoulder of my hoodie. "C'mon!" she said.

"What are you . . . ?" I sputtered.

"Come on!" she insisted. She was still pulling me by the shoulder of my sweatshirt, talking so fast I could barely follow all that she was saying. Something about her friend Jenna's dad being the advisor of the year-book staff and really cool digital cameras with big zoom lenses. . . . It was all I could do just to keep up with Kate and stay on my feet.

A couple of minutes later Kate pulled me through the door of the yearbook room and she introduced me to Mr. Billings, Jenna's dad. Mr. Billings seemed as confused as me, until Kate pulled the camera from the top of my backpack and began showing him the pictures I had taken that weekend at Hickory Grove Lake.

"You're in sixth grade, Toni?" Mr. Billings asked.

"Yes, sir," I answered.

"Do you take a lot of pictures?" he asked.

"I guess so," I said. "I got that camera for Christmas last year."

"Your pictures are very good," he said.

I was shocked. I never think anything I do or make is good, other than on a ball field, that is.

"Have you ever used one of these?" he asked. He went to his desk and brought out a bigger, professional-looking camera. It had an actual lens on the front that could be focused, and then he showed me an even bigger lens that was used for taking close-up photos. He showed me how to focus and how to change out the lenses.

"So what do you say? Do I have a new photographer for the yearbook?" he asked with a smile.

"Really?" I asked. "You would let me have this camera?"

"Well, it's more *use* than *have*," he said. "Deal?"

"Deal!" I said.

"You'll need your first assignment then," Mr. Billings said. He shuffled through some slips of paper scattered across his desk. "Ah, this one looks perfect," he said.

And Mr. Billings handed me my first photographic assignment ever. I could sense the importance of the moment, almost like it would play a big part in my future someday. Who knows? I could win the Pulitzer Prize and be really famous if I am as good as Kate and Mr. Billings think I am. With a deep breath I smiled and looked down at my future:

Assignment: Junior high football practice, this Thursday.

CHAPTER 10

Where I Belong

"They can't make me do it!" I said.

Mrs. V stayed quiet, waiting for me to go on.

"What do I do now?" I asked.

"Well," Mrs. V said, "I suppose you could take the camera back and tell Mr. Billings that you won't be able to take pictures for him today after all."

I shook my head. "I can't do that. He's depending on me. Why can't I just take pictures of the marching band, or the cross-country team?"

"Maybe there is a reason you are supposed to go to the football field," she said.

"Like what?" I pouted.

"Unfinished business?" Mrs. V said with a smile.

"I'd rather wear a tutu and become a ballet dancer than finish any business with Trevor Kenworth," I said.

"And what if your business isn't with Trevor?" Mrs. V asked.

She hopped up on the tall countertop behind her desk and pushed aside a bunch of crispy papers that had been left there by her watercolor class. With one easy jump I joined her.

"Why aren't you playing soccer, Toni?" Mrs. V asked.

"I don't know," I said, staring at our dangling feet. "Maybe girls just shouldn't play sports."

"Do you really think that?" she asked.

"I don't like it when people say I can't do something because I'm a girl," I said quietly.

Mrs. V kind of made a humming noise and then she was quiet for a while. "I tried out for a few teams when I was in school," she finally said. "Didn't make any of them."

"Which ones?" I asked her.

"Let's see." She thought for a moment. "In middle school I was cut from basketball and softball. In high school I tried out for gymnastics and soccer." She shrugged. "I tried, but it just wasn't who I was created to be."

"Wow," I said. "That's a lot of times to get cut."

"Oh yeah." She smiled. "I was a pro at getting cut!"

"But you're really great at art," I said, hoping to make her feel better.

"Yep, I'm pretty great at art." She smiled. And then I knew what she was saying. I'm pretty great at sports—not pretty great for a girl, but just pretty great, period.

I looked at the clock on Mrs. V's wall. Three fifteen. If I hurried I could make it just in time.

Halfway across the room I realized I forgot something. I ran back to Mrs. V and threw my arms around her neck. "Thanks, Mrs. V," I said. "You're the *best!*"

I took a deep breath as I approached the track around the football field. Was it really only three days ago that Yuzi and I created the world's greatest mascot disaster *ever*—right here on this very ground? Across the field I could see the team gathering to take a knee around Coach. He saw me and waved me over.

Oh great. Mr. Billings must have told him I'm coming. I put my head down and began the long walk across the field. The wind has been picking up lately and there's a new chill in the air. Fall is definitely just around the corner.

I heard the boys begin to clap their hands. One clap, then another, and another . . . the claps were picking up speed and getting louder. And the guys were saying something . . . what was it?

Stone?

Phone?

Tone? Toni?

Toni! That was it! They were saying my name, and clapping, cheering, waving towels in the air. Then I really had to look twice. It sure looked like the guy standing next to Coach Klutz was . . . my **dad**?

Beast and Smitty couldn't wait any longer. They grabbed something off the table behind them and came running at me. I stopped in my tracks when I saw what it was.

A green football jersey. Number fifty-one. The name Diaz was printed in neat block letters across the back.

"We thought you'd never get here, Diaz," said Smitty.

"Yeah." Beast grinned. "Man, it takes girls *forever* to get ready!"

"Wha—What's this?" I stammered.

Smitty laughed and clapped me on the shoulder. "We have an opening for a kicker, if you think you can handle the job."

I must have looked totally confused. "What about Trevor?" I asked.

"He got in trouble or something." Beast shrugged.

"Besides, your foot is the one we've always wanted," said Smitty. "Dude, no other middle school in the whole *county* has anyone who can boot the ball like you."

My dad and Coach wandered out to where we stood. They were both grinning from ear to ear.

"Did you hear, Daddy?" I knew it was a dumb question, but I didn't know what else to say.

"I heard." My dad smiled.

Coach Klutz started explaining what was going on. "The yearbook advisor told me at lunch today that he was sending a nice young lady named Toni Diaz—one of his best, he said—out to photograph our practice today. It took some doing, but we thought we'd use that information to our advantage and give you a proper welcome to the team."

"Wow." I was speechless. "But Dad said . . ."

"I called your dad after Trevor left the team," said Coach. "I said, 'Albert, did you see your daughter kick that ball at mascot tryouts Monday?'"

My dad put his arm around Coach Klutz and laughed. "And I said, 'It's *Alberto*, and yes, I saw. She's been kicking like that since she was in her mom's belly.'"

Usually it really embarrasses me when my dad says that—it's so lame. But today, for some reason it made me cry.

"So . . . does that mean . . . I can *play*?" I asked nervously.

I looked to my dad. Our eyes kind of locked together for a second and then he put his hands on my shoulders. "First things first, Toni," he said. "You are still grounded for three weeks. *Comprende?* You come straight home after football."

"Yes, sir," I said. I know my dad. He finishes everything that he starts.

My dad smiled down at me. "When I spoke with Coach Klutz, he told me something I already knew, Toni. You're a natural athlete. You're strong. You're quick and you're a great team player. So, I decided we should give it a shot. . . . You aren't like every other girl, and that's what makes you *my* Toni. Plus, he promised me that he would watch out for you and make sure nobody disrespected you in any way."

I threw my arms around my dad and felt him pick me up about two feet off the ground. Then—I don't know **what** I was thinking—I threw my arms around Coach. When I looked at Smitty he just said, "Don't even think about it, Diaz," and he gave me a high five.

And I guess my surprises were not over yet, because at that moment both Milo and Marcos came running onto the field wearing green jerseys with #51 on the front and "T Diaz" across the back. They stopped in front of Smitty and Beast, absolutely towering over the two biggest boys on the middle school football team.

"You two lead this team, right?" Milo said. "Well, if our little sister plays on this team, *you* had better make sure she's treated like a Princess. *Got it?*"

"And just to make sure you're doing your job," Marcos growled, "we'll be at every single game."

Smitty and Beast snapped to attention and saluted my brothers like they were in the army or something, but I could see a huge awestruck smile in their eyes.

Running to put my camera bag down on the bench, I spied my best buds leaning against the track fence.

"Toni, come here!" Danika was jumping up and down with a goofy smile on her face. She had something pink in her hands . . .

Kate couldn't stand the excitement. "Cleats! They're for you!" She giggled and pointed to the shiny pink football shoes that Danika was holding high above her head.

Yuzi grabbed the shoes from Danika and thrust them

into my hands. They were perfect. Pink with white stripes, a big T for Antonia on the tongue of the shoe, the number 51 in rhinestones on the side of the shoe and on the heel . . .

"No way," I whispered. "The secret shark sign. Did you draw this, Yuzi?"

"I had a little help from Beast and Smitty, but you betcha. That was me!"

"Did you know about this yesterday?" I asked Kate.

"Nope," she said. "Neither did Mr. Billings. Mrs. V found out at lunch today and told us. We called Danika's dad 'cause he has a friend who makes custom shoes."

"Yuzi worked like mad to get those ready," Danika said, nearly choking poor Yuzi with an enthusiastic hug.

"You ready, Diaz?" Coach asked from behind me.

"I've been ready all my life," I said, giving my girl-friends high fives all around.

My dad gave me one last hug. "I love you, Princess," he whispered into my ear. Then he jumped the fence to join the girls.

"I love you, Daddy," I said. "Tell Mom I said thanks." It was then I remembered my new job—I had been sent here to take pictures, after all.

"Group picture!" I shouted, grabbing my on-loan camera from its bag.

Danika, Yuzi, and Kate, like they all had one mind or something, immediately jumped on the chain-link fence and struck monkey poses. I wasn't shocked, but my buds just about lost it when my dad and brothers jumped on the fence too, hanging by one hand and making chimpanzee faces. I had to take three pictures before I got one that was in focus. We were all laughing so hard.

I placed the camera carefully in its bag and with one last look of contentment at my best friends—my very own Secret Keepers—I jogged across the cool, newly cut grass, back to where I belong.

They Can't Stop Me!

Girl Gab About the YOU that God Created!

Hey Secret Keeper Girl! I hope you had a good time getting to know Toni Diaz. Have you ever felt like her? Have you ever struggled with how God created you—to be athletic, a bookworm, the life of the party, super-adventurous, or whatever? Maybe you've wondered if life might be a little easier if you could be just like the other girls. Actually, God's Word says that'd be pretty bad.

Check out 1 Corinthians 12:14-18

Now the body is not made up of one part but of many. If the foot should say, "Because I am not a hand, I do not belong to the body," it would not for that reason cease to be part of the body. And if the ear should say, "Because I am not an eye, I do not belong to the body," it would not for that reason cease to be part of the body. If the whole body were an eye, where would the sense of hearing be? If the whole body were an ear, where would the sense of smell be? But in fact God has arranged the parts in the body, every one of them, just as he wanted them to be.

Gab About It:

❧ Let's imagine we—you, me, and all the rest of the world—make up the parts of a body. It'd be pretty nuts if we were all "eyes" on a body and there were no mouths or hands or feet. Why are *all* the parts of the body important? ....

....

....

....

❧ According to this verse, who gets to decide what role each part of the body performs? ....

....

....

....

❧ OK, think about something you do really well. Maybe it's football like Toni or maybe it's matching up clothes or passing math with flying colors. OK, now, *who* decided to make you that way? ....

....

....

....

💕 Have you ever tried out for or done something just to be with friends or to be like someone else? Has your mom? Share your stories and have a good giggle together. ....

....

....

....

💕 Why do you think the roles of mascot and of actress don't work out very well for Toni?...

....

....

....

💕 How does Mrs. V's personal story about school tryouts help Toni at the start of chapter 10? ....

....

....

....

PRAY IT OUT LOUD!

You know what would be pretty cool about right now? What if your mom told you all of the gifts she sees at work in your life— all of the things that you do and say and express really well—and then she prayed for those gifts to keep growing and growing in your life? And she can also pray that, like Toni, you bravely embrace who you are created to be!

"T" is for Antonia